A NOTE TO PARENTS

Young children can be overwhelmed by their emotions—often because they don't understand and can't express what they are feeling. This, in turn, can frustrate parents. After all, how can you help your child deal with a problem if you don't even share a common vocabulary?

Welcome to HOW i FEEL —a series designed to bridge this communication gap. With simple text, lively illustrations, and an interactive format, each book describes familiar situations to help children recognize a particular emotion. It gives them a vocabulary to talk about what they're feeling, and it offers practical suggestions for dealing with those feelings.

Each time you read this book with your child, you can reinforce the message with one of the following activities:

- Ask your child to make up a story about a little girl or boy who is frustrated.

- Play a game of pretend to act out a situation that frustrates your child.

- Explore different causes of frustration—and possible solutions—with the "I Feel Frustrated!" activity card and reusable stickers included with this book.

I hope you enjoy the HOW i FEEL series and that it will help your child take the first solid steps toward understanding emotions.

Marcia Leonard

Executive Producers: John Christianson and Ron Berry
Art Design: Gary Currant
Layout: Currant Design Group and Best Impression Graphics

HOW i FEEL

FRUSTRATED

by Marcia Leonard
illustrated by Bartholomew

This little girl is trying to hit the ball,
but she keeps missing.
She feels frustrated.

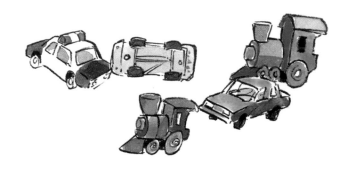

This little boy is frustrated, too.
He just started to play,
and now his dad says
it's time to go.

This little girl is frustrated because
she's having trouble getting dressed.

Has that ever happened to you?
Can you make a face
that looks frustrated?

Everyone feels frustrated at times.
It can happen when you try
something new.

Do you like to try new things?

It can happen when you're not quite
old enough or big enough to do
what you want to do.

Is there something
that you're too little to do?

If you feel frustrated, it's a good idea
to stop what you're doing,
take a deep breath and let it out slowly,
and try to calm down.

You can do something else for a while.

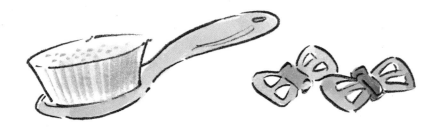

You can ask someone to help you.

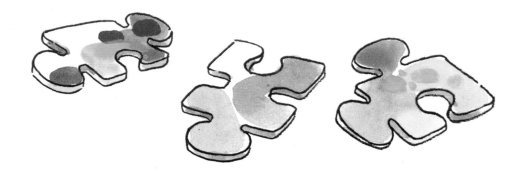

Or, if you feel ready,
you can try again.

The good news is, as you grow older,
you'll get better and better
at doing lots of things.
Then you won't feel frustrated so often.

I FEEL FRUSTRATED!
Instructions

Use this activity to help your child identify—and explore solutions to—a variety of frustrating experiences. Remove the card and reusable stickers from the back pocket of the book. Ask your child to choose one of the stickers representing a typically frustrating experience and place it in the left-hand column of the chart. Then ask him or her to choose a sticker representing a possible response to that experience and place it in the right-hand column. If your child wants to choose more than one response sticker, that's fine. When the stickers are in place, they will make a complete sentence. Read it out loud; then talk to your child about the choices he or she made.